East To West

The Copper Bridge

author Dolores Kruzona

illustrator Christina Bethoney-Whitten

First Published by Quill & Grace Publishing 2020

ISBN: 978-1-7342588-0-6

Printed in the United States of America

I would like to dedicate this book to my younger sister, Christina. She inspired, supported, and had faith in me and my story, which is her heritage as well.
I am truly grateful for her hard work.
Dolores Kruzona

The women of the great immigration era were brave beyond belief. They rolled up their sleeves and worked hard.

These women worked endlessly; did all that was needed and required, for their families and so much more.

So many generous women; they never forgot to share with those around them who needed help, though they had so little themselves.

These women had great courage! They raised their families with dignity and real faith in God.

This story is written for them. Most of it is true. I remember hearing it from conversations around the family table.

Their "Old Country" traditional recipes and breads continue on even today, included in our everyday meals, holiday meals, and special occasions.
Dolores Kruzona

Table of Contents

CHAPTER 1

Our New Beginning in America

N a'am put both apple pies into the oven. She whispered a little prayer that they would make a filling supper. The table was covered with old newspapers, cores, and peelings. Na'am noticed a bit of sugar in a little pile near the center of the table where one of the papers sat. She very carefully scooped it up, and she re-opened the oven to scatter it on the top of one of the pies. She knew that both pies could have used a lot more sugar and cinnamon, but there wasn't anymore. She had grated some of the outer peel of the one precious lemon left onto the apples for flavor, to make up for the lack of sugar. She would have used more, but the lemon was going to become cold lemonade combined with a bit of honey put into a glass jug, then into the ice-box for when Joseph came home. He would be hot and tired. It would satisfy him until they could all sit down together for their supper.

Mr. Joe had come by the back door that morning with a bushel of apples. He knew Na'am would take them. He only charged her fifteen cents. They both knew that the bottom layer would be rotten. The fifteen cents was better than throwing them away. He would get a good price from his other customers who would go through whole boxes searching to replace a single bad apple, before they would buy. He would charge them much more, of course. But it was an unwritten agreement that Na'am would take the bushel without a word, and he knew that she would be happy to have them. She would clean, core, and bake with the spotted ones. The few good apples would be washed and polished dry for her children, to eat from their lunch pails. The very best one would be saved for Joseph; her husband.

But Mr. Joe's real reason for coming by as often as possible was because Na'am would offer him a cold glass of water and a thick slice of her warm bread, without fail. It was just like his dear mother's bread. He missed her and the smell of her kitchen where he grew up as a boy in Russia. He had to leave her there alone, to seize his chance to come to America when he was seventeen. She sent him off gladly, because she knew it was his chance for a good life. There was nothing for poor people in Russia except hard work and often starvation. He was forty now and he would never see his sweet mama again. She had died when he was thirty-two. He had promised her he would come back home and bring her to America to live. He never had enough for the fares that he would have needed to travel back and forth, until now. But, it was too late. Na'am's bread was more than a slice of bread to him.

Joseph, Na'am's husband, had been teaching three classes a week, at the university, for two months now. He taught Middle Eastern History to freshmen. Joseph had to take two buses to get there and walked two and a half miles to come home. He was saving the return fare home to help pay for Mary Rose's school coat. She would need it before winter came. Joseph had a bad heart. The doctor said there was an operation, he had heard of being done in a Boston hospital now. Of course, that was impossible for Joseph. That kind of treatment was available only for the rich.

Their eldest daughter Jennie lived in Boston with her husband, Tom. They had fallen in love aboard the ship that brought them to freedom. She was only seventeen, but there was no stopping them. Tom was handsome and strong. He had come from a village, a day's walk away. Joseph had known the family well. It was a good family. Jennie had long, shining, chestnut hair and a brilliant smile. The priest, one of a group traveling to America, happily married them on a lovely, sunny morning, on the upper deck. The cook had treated their family to a small cake and tea. He too, liked to look at Jennie. As the couple danced around and around, to accordion music the cook sighed. The bride and groom were happy about their new life and now would share the great adventure together.

Joseph and Na'am knew that their daughter and Tom didn't have very much and were living with Tom's mother in an apartment. Jennie took good care of Tom's mother tenderly caring for her as if she were her own. Both youngsters worked very hard in the factory, which was a hearty walk of four blocks from their apartment. They held hands as they walked briskly each morning. They took very good care of the old mother who could still get around in the house, but tired easily. No, Joseph and Na'am would not ask anything of them. Life was hard enough for Jennie and Tom. They were happy and looking forward to having a nicer place and raising children one day soon.

Naaj, their oldest boy had quit high school in his junior year to help out his family. His mother was very angry about that. Naaj went to work in the Shenandoah coal mines because there was no other work. At least it paid the mortgage on the house. Naaj hated the hard work. It was dirty he thought, and demeaning. No one should have to go under the ground to work! He knew his father and mother were nearly desperate to keep them with food and clothing. They would one day own their own house free and clear. But they had to make the payments, faithfully. People were being tossed onto the streets by the banks, after missing only one payment. Naaj vowed that would not happen to them, if he could help it, and worse, it would shame their family.

Millie helped too. She worked in a hat shop. Sometimes she received a tip from a grand looking lady, who wore a fox fur. She came in very often and took a liking to Millie. However, Millie would spend her tip on a little bonnet for herself, after they shut the doors, to the shop for the day. After all she deserved it, didn't she? Most of her pay went to her mother. It bought the yeast and flour for breakfast bread. Sometimes, it bought milk and some vegetables in the winter. Millie knew that a dozen girls would jump at the chance to have her job. She became especially careful to do a good job in keeping it. She swept up the floors after hours. Millie washed the front windows, before the owner, Mrs. Janeski put in the new display for the month. She was always careful to put the colorful pink and gold trimmed bonnets up front. Mrs. Alda Wadsworth was partial to those colors. Mrs.Wadsworth was the tipper. Millie always ran two doors down to the tea shop to bring her back some hot tea, whenever she came in to try on bonnets. If she were not too hungry she would take her slice of Na'am's bread, from her lunch pail and place it on a bit of white linen. She would carefully put it by Mrs. Wadsworth's cup of tea. It would always result in a tip. Mrs. Wadsworth would not leave the crust or even the crumbs. Millie tucked one quarter of her two quarter tip, into her purse.

The first quarter was for a bonnet, which would not sell. It was destined for the backroom bin anyway. It would be used to re-work its bits and pieces onto some other bonnet, which would then go into the front window again, until it sold. Mrs. Janeski didn't mind selling it to Millie, for the quarter and it was good advertisement. Millie wore them so well. She was a very pretty girl.

Millie was clever about these bonnets. She would buy one a week and try to sell it to one of her girlfriends who would surely, admire it. If she were not able to sell it, she would proudly wear it to church. Every Sunday she would wear a different one. Someone would ask her, after church if she could buy it on the sly. Many a pretty hat went to church, and many a pretty quarter went into Millie's pocket. Most were kept for a Saturday night, some were for her mother. Mother was very grateful, thinking they were Millie's tips. She bought many of the apples and vegetables from Mr. Joe, for her family.

Millie would drop the extra quarters into her purse, very carefully. Saturday night rolled around pretty quickly. Sometimes it was movie night. Sometimes it would be dance night if Mary Rose would not pester her, to go along to the movies. Millie really hated that. She couldn't flirt with the boys, if Mary Rose were tagging along. If she could only get out the door, without her she could meet her girlfriends. They would go dancing and if she had a good week financially, she would even treat her friends to smokes. She prayed her Mother would never find out. Millie was clever and after all they were her tips. She worked very hard for them.

Toffie knew! He would see his sister at Roxie's most Saturday nights. He never told on her. But, he always watched out for her. Toffie was a great dancer. He loved to go dancing on Saturday nights. He had finished high school. He was free to go into the Army if he chose. His Mother begged him not to join. She prayed every night on her knees, that he would not go. For now, he got up every morning and put on his freshly washed pants and warm jersey neatly laid out for him. He took his jacket off the peg by the door, picked up his equipment in the back closet under the steps, and go to work in the coal mines, with Naaj. He didn't like it, but he didn't hate it as his brother did. He just accepted it, after all Saturday night would be coming along

Saturday night did come. He would steal a little yellow mum from one of Na'am's flower pots, on the kitchen window sill and place it, in the button hole of his church jacket. Whistling and clicking a few dance steps he would leave to pick up his date, to go dancing at the Roxie. It was the highlight of his day, his week, his life. Dancing set him free. He was graceful and handsome on the dance floor. Waltzing was his favorite dance. He knew he was handsome, with a little, clean-cut mustache and a sweet smile. The girls would practically swoon when he would give the kids "a break" and pick the homeliest girl, who would hide in the corner waiting in pain, for the end of the dance. When Toffie came in their poor little hearts would jump for joy. It meant that one or two of them would dance that night. Perhaps one of them would be a princess for the night. Although he tried never to dance twice with anyone. That would be mean and give her false hope. He knew this. Sometimes he would find the same girl sitting in the corner the next week, and he could not help himself. He would want to draw her out, into the light and joy of the dance. So he would ask again, but not often. His own date would be waiting; not too patiently.

So there they were, Na'am and Joseph's children. And then too, there was Mary Rose. Mary Rose was their youngest child born in America. They all loved her very much. Na'am loved her with all her heart. Mary Rose was the sweetest. She did not have a mean bone in her. Na'am loved combing her long, black hair and using the hot tongs to bring her hair, into long, bouncing curls every morning for school. Mary Rose was sweet and good. She helped her mother as much as she could. She loved to work in her mother's warm, clean kitchen, where she could always find her. Mary Rose would put her arms around her mom and smell her cleanliness. She would kiss her cheek lightly and dance her in a circle before being told to "mind now."

Na'am shared her secrets with Mary Rose. Whispering her story to Mary Rose, Na'am told her about what it was like when she was just a little peasant girl working in the fields, in the "old country." How one day she saw a handsome boy on a beautiful, white horse go riding, by her father's field. Na'am thought him wonderful. She watched that boy ride by every day. One evening there was a knock at her father's door. Standing there in front of her was the ruler of the town they all lived near. The boy Na'am had been watching was the son of the ruler; a prince. The boy's father was a prince! He sat down in the special chair meant for company. A strong liquor, clear and sweet was brought out of the cupboard, by Na'am's mother. Also, along with delicious, fresh bread were washed and neatly cut vegetables. Slices of her own good cheese were all offered to the prince, on a clean coarse cloth unfolded and carefully spread, before the men on a little wooden table. They sat by the fire to eat and drink.

The women were sent to the far side of the room. The men had the right to speak of many important things, without their presence. Na'am's older sister Raja let her hide her face, in her skirt because she was frightened." Raja whispered, "Be calm. It is not for bad, but for good, that he is here."

Na'ams father called her to him shortly afterwards. He took her hand and asked his wife how many years she had in his house. Mother said, "She has only 14 years my husband." He sent his wife away again. The prince looked at Na'am kindly and asked "Are you a good girl?" Na'am blushed and lowered her eyes. Then she said, "Sir, my Father must answer for me." Na'am was sent back to the other side of the room, to sit by her mother and sister far from the conversation going on.

Na'am's mother was called over to them again. Father said, "Mother, the Prince says your bread is most good! You must bake him seven loaves every week." "Yes, my husband," said Na'am's mother. She then threw her apron over her face and left the men to sit by Na'am and Raja.

"Why did your mother do that," asked Mary Rose. Na'am explained saying, "That was a great honor for my Mother. She covered her face so as to hide her pride, from God and man."

In one year, Na'am was married to Joseph. Her father received many gifts. It was wonderful to see her father's happiness as he rode a new, little donkey to market. It was wonderful to have many blocks of cheese wrapped in clean cloths, against the winter hunger.

Na'am loved Joseph and he loved her. He took her to live in his father's fine house for many happy years. But their happiness was not forever. Some very frightening news came to the town. Very important news! It struck fear in every home, and every heart of these simple and good people.

12

Na'am and Joseph were made to run away, in the bright early dawn, by their old parents. Their gold pieces were hidden in Na'am's kerchief and Joseph's belt. They now had two sons and two daughters to think about. The prince paid their passage and the passage of a few other families, from his clan. The enemy soldiers were coming soon to every village to "steal" the young men for their army. No one was to be exempted. The prince left for his hidden mountain home high up in the hills. He took as many families as he could. It was only a matter of time. He sent those who had the younger sons among their immediate families, over the fields to the city where they could get safe passage to America. All the while keeping secret their few gold coins.

Na'am had wrapped and tied their few belongings into a beautiful, butter colored, crocheted bedspread on which her mother had taught her all the various stitches. All that her mother had taught her was in her mind and heart. It was a treasure trove taught with love and respect, to both her daughters. She had nothing else to give them. Still Na'am cried and when she could cry no longer she then cried in her heart. In the last moments her mother gave her a small package wrapped, in a piece of white cloth. She told her to hide it carefully and not to open it until they were safely, on the ship. She hugged her and smiled through her tears. Then she turned away from her sweet younger daughter and walked towards her husband and older daughter Raja. She had begged Raja to go to America with her husband and little sons, but Raja would not leave her parents not even for freedom. The village people prepared to leave with the prince, who was patiently waiting, with his family all of whom were on beautiful horses. All his townspeople began to walk with

13

them towards the hidden, back country, up into the hills. Na'am's mother and father did not look back.

Mary Rose loved the story of her mother and father's courtship and early married years. It was like a fairy tale. She knew they had suffered much. They came to Shenandoah, Pennsylvania not knowing the language or customs of America. Na'am worked hard. It was all she knew to do. She took in other folks wash. Everyone loved her because she was honest and straight, in everything she did. Joseph went to school to learn the language. He had taught school in his villa, before they had married. He was already very learned. He soon passed the test to teach here, in his new country. He loved to read and teach history. He was recognized among his peers and after years was invited, to teach at the university.

Of course that changed somewhat when he was diagnosed with his heart ailment. Joseph had to work less. He now taught three classes a week. Every seat was taken. The school didn't mind having a top notch teacher who worked only 3 classes a week. It saved them money yet, it gave the school some prestige.

Na'am was worried about Joseph. She knew he was brought up with fine things and fine foods and good care. This America while blessed by freedom, was harsh and hard on him. She saw his handsome face begin to age early. She saw his fine mustache become gray. She tried very hard to shield him from everything, but this was impossible. She watched her children grow and go to work, in the mines. It was a hateful thing to her. Her beautiful sons entering those awful, underground mines. The town people always watched to make sure the managers took the canary cages down first. It was their only safety measure. The birds would die first if the poisoned air seeped, into the caves. The workers always watched for running rats down, in the mines, another safe guard for "cave-in" warnings. It was a dangerous and thankless place to work.

Mary Rose sat in her room crying hard. Her teacher had hit her again. She kept on slapping her face, while holding onto her long curls. She was after all a freshman in high school. She did quite well in school. She just could not understand her teacher's anger, almost every day. This teacher was unkind to many students, but she had taken a particular dislike to this simple, sweet girl. Perhaps it was for that reason alone, as Mary Rose was a good student. Her love of school was quickly turning, into a daily, fearful, nightmare.

Na'am, finishing up the kitchen work, had gone into the wash room, to set the wash to soaking. It had to be bright and clean as Mrs.Tabinski was very fussy about her husband's shirts being really bright, and really white! He was after all a businessman. Na'am suddenly raised her head as she thought she heard crying. She walked into Mary Roses' room without knocking. "My child what has happened to you?" "Why are you crying my sweet girl?" "Mother, please forgive me. I did not mean to make you trouble." "What! What has happened, tell me now?" Mary Rose told her mother. She did not know how to lie. Her cheeks were still red, from the slaps she endured that afternoon.

Na'am took off her apron. She quickly reached up to the shelf, in the kitchen and put on her black, church hat. She still had a smudge of flour on her face. She did not change her house dress. She grasped Mary Rose by the hand and pushed her ahead and out of the door. They did not realize their house door was left standing open. Na'am walked quickly down the street towards the school. It was three blocks away. Na'am did not slow her pace for a moment. Mary Rose was out of breath, but not her mother.

Na'am marched up the stone stairs and flung the two front doors wide open. She paused to have Mary Rose point out her home room. Na'am pushed Mary Rose down on the bench, outside that door. She walked into the school room where the teacher was sitting, at her desk working on some papers. Another young lady was seated, in the corner facing the wall. Mrs. Warren stood up at the sight of Na'am, with a half smile frozen on her face. Na'am never lost her temper, but today she was crazed with anger. She told the young lady to come out of the corner...."Go home young lady; you are not a child!" She ran! She was afraid, but oh, so happy, to be free from the wrath of Mrs. Warren. After all, she had only dropped her pencil while Mrs. Warren was talking. She didn't mean to do that.

Na'am grabbed the teacher by her blouse front and put her little face right up into Mrs. Warren's face. "You never, never strike my girl's face again!" She spoke in a low, tense, controlled voice. She had an accent however, her words were quite clear. "You never, never touch my girl again! You never, never strike any child again! I will come back to you! I will come back to you!"

She dropped Mrs. Warren back into her chair with a wild shove. She brushed her hands together as if she could not bear the touch of Mrs. Warren's clothes. She then turned around and marched out. Mary Rose followed her mother at a trot, out the two huge wooden doors of the school, down the stone stairs and at a fast pace back down the three blocks to her home. Her mother placed her Sunday hat back, on the high shelf. She put her apron on and walked into the laundry room, to finish the wash. It must be ready by the next afternoon for Mrs.Tabinski. She still had to line dry them in the sunshine. Mary Rose was astounded. She had never seen her mother so angry, not in her whole life.

Mary Rose was very proud of her mother. She went into the wash room and shyly lifted her eyes, to her mother's eyes. "Mama, Thank you".....Na'am began to weep. As she wiped her eyes with the corner of Mr. Tabinski's shirt. She said, "My child, no one has the right to strike you, but your father or your mother. This we have never done and never will. You children are our wealth and our treasure, in this life. Mary Rose you are my heart!" Mary Rose stood as still as stone, realizing this afternoon had cost her mother much. She was crying from her heart, deep within. Every corner of the house was still.

Joseph called out: "Peace be to this house." Joseph was home at last. "Run my child and take your father's hat and case. We must get him the cold lemonade and let him rest now." Na'am was herself again. She straightened her back and walked out to answer her husband with "Peace be to you my husband."

Many people were out of work now. Some in Shenandoah would not allow their sons to go into the mines. These families suffered tremendously and some even lost their houses. A few went back to the "old country" and some went to the cities, to try to find some work. Some folks went to live with other relatives and some families disbanded in order to exist as best they could. Their men and boys took to begging, or riding the rails. Times were very hard.

Millie thought the bonnet shop might close before long. She wanted to get in as many Saturday nights as possible. She knew it would be difficult to find an extra quarter or two, if she lost her job. Movies and dances would be out of the question. She was glad to give her pay to her mother. She knew it went to help feed them. But her tips were hers.

Mary Rose wanted to go to the movies, with her this Saturday night. She didn't have an extra quarter for her and smokes too. "No, Mary Rose, you can't go with me." "Oh Millie, I want to go out too, it's been a hard week for me." "No, no, no! You are not going with me."

Mary Rose knew that Na'am had a mason jar, with some coins in it. Mother kept it in the corner of the cupboard above the old black, cast iron stove. Mary never saw her mother put money in it, nor did she see her ever take money out of it. Mary pulled the little three legged stool, over to the stove. She climbed up on it being careful not to disturb the rising bread dough, on the back of the stove. She took the mason jar down to the table. Inside were three quarters, three nickels, and a dozen pennies. Surely one quarter would not be missed. Father came into the kitchen to warm his feet near the stove. He seemed to feel the cold a bit more lately.

"Mary Rose, what would mother say to you, I am shocked to see you steal." "Oh Father, shut up!" Mary Rose cried out. Father stared at Mary Rose not believing his ears. His face flushed red. His eyes closed in shame and sorrow. As soon as Mary Rose heard her own words to her father, she could have died of shame. "Oh Papa, I didn't mean it, Oh Papa forgive me, please, I didn't even know what I was saying." Papa, "Forgive me! Forgive me!" Mary Rose dropped the mason jar to the floor. The change spilled out across the linoleum floor. Father turned away, without a word and went into his bedroom. He quietly shut the door.

Mary Rose sat down on the kitchen chair. She covered her face with her hands and shook all over. How could she have been so cruel, so disrespectful to her father. After a little while, Father came out to the kitchen. He placed two quarters on the table. He told Mary Rose to pick up all the change that had fallen and to put it back where her mother had kept it. Mary Rose said, "Father how can I take this. I am so ashamed and so sorry! Please, can you forgive me?" Father Joseph said in his quiet voice, with tears in his eyes, "Mary Rose you must take it. How else can you forgive me and I forgive you? Obey me now." Mary Rose came over to her father and grasped his right hand and kissed the back if it, so tenderly. It was the ritual of the "old country" a begging for forgiveness. She had seen her brothers do this once or twice. Her father smiled at her. He went back into his room.

The laundry room floor creaked. Na'am had seen and heard all. She shut the door. Mary Rose was alone.

It was Saturday morning at last. It seemed Na'am gave them less chores today. Her young sons and daughters were puzzled. What would make their mother hurry so? When the afternoon was still young, she said to Millie, Mary Rose, Toffie and Naaj, "Hurry children wash up and put on fresh shirts and blouses." Na'am hurried to do the same. Even father was busy brushing his hair. They looked at one another, however, all did as they were told. There was no question about that.

Na'am hurried down the front steps, with her family quickly following her. Father took her arm in his, so proudly. Soon they were at church and all sitting, in the last pew by the confessional. "It is long overdue," said Na'am. It's what is wrong with all of us." She went in to the confessional first. When she was finished she walked to the front pew, before the Holy Tabernacle to say a penance. She was radiant with joy. Her lovely face had a light of peace on it.

Afterwards they all walked home, peace filling their hearts, they sat around the supper table. Na'am put a beautiful, little wooden crucifix on the table. It had been rewrapped in the same old, white linen her mother had given her years before. There were three tiny rubies where the heart of Jesus was pierced. Na'am wanted to put the crucifix up on the wall in a place of honor, but it must be their choice of where it was to hang.

Mother, "Where did this come from," they cried? "My mother took it down from the wall of my home in the "old country." It was her mother's and her mother's before her. It has been hidden away far too long. If Jesus is honored in our home things will go much better. We won't be afraid anymore to be kind to one another."

So the beautiful, little, brown, hand-carved crucifix was hung up in the living room where they could not fail to see it, on approaching the room. They all felt happy again. Soon they were eating supper, laughing, talking, and enjoying each other's company, as they always had before.

Mary Rose was going to the "Roxie" after all. Toffie was going to take her with him. He gave Mary Rose a few rules: Don't leave the dance with anyone but me. Don't dance with anyone that I signal "no" to you and don't drink or smoke anything. I will bring you something to drink myself and save a couple dances for me. "Ok, ok, Toffie, I will do anything you ask me to, I promise." Mary Rose wore her navy blue dress, with the white collar. Her mother tied a light blue ribbon in her hair lifting her curls, to the back of her head. She was beautiful.

Was she seeing things? She stood by the wall watching Toffie and Naaj on the dance floor. Toffie would dance with a different girl every dance. Naaj was asking the same pretty girl, with the flowered dress and very long, blond hair, flowing loose, to dance again and again. They did the polka. They waltzed. They slow danced, too. But, Naan didn't change partners and he held her a bit close. Mary Rose tried not to watch, but she could not help seeing Naaj's face. It was quite intent. The blond girl pretended not to see it. She just wanted to dance. She wanted the other girls to notice that Naaj, that other handsome boy with the accent just wanted to dance with her. She tossed her long hair again and again, as she twirled across the dance floor. Toffie never asked her to dance. Naaj always did, every time he came to the "Roxie." But, tonight he didn't leave her side. Soon Mary Rose forgot about Naaj and the blond girl, as she was dancing herself. As soon as the boys realized there was a new girl and she could really dance well, she was made to dance with each one. They wouldn't let her sit out one dance. Toffie came to her rescue, but not to rest. He danced with Mary Rose too. They knew each other's steps so well. They made a pretty sight and soon people were clapping. Mary Rose was flushed with the dancing and excitement.

"Oh Toffie, I had such a good time, thank you! You are a good brother, and a good friend too...thank you!" They were sprawled on the living room couch, shoes off and laughing about everything. Their mother came out of the bedroom to join them. Soon Naaj and Millie would be home and they too would join, in the conversation and the fun. Mary Rose asked Toffie who the blond girl was? "She is Geraldine Walena, and she is a real show off! No one takes her seriously, but she is a good dancer." "Well, I think Naaj was!" Mary Rose spoke without thinking and her mother sat up straight, but said nothing, an odd look on her face. Soon the others came in and all were laughing and recounting the stories of the night, once again. Mother looked carefully at Naaj. He was flushed and excited too, more than she had seen him ever before.

After mass the next morning mother said to them, "Father and I are going for a little walk by ourselves. Please go home and make some breakfast. We will be home soon." This was strange. Mother and father always went right home to make breakfast for them all. They watched as their parents walked towards the middle of town where there was a little park. They could see them sit down on a bench still deep in conversation.

Naaj was going to be married. It was all arranged. Joseph said she was from a very good family in Scranton. She had four brothers and a sister. Three of the brothers were going to school, at the university where Joseph taught. Joseph had known their father in the "old country." He had come to America with lots of gold pieces, to get them started. He had done very well in his adopted country. One of his sons was studying to be a doctor and one was studying to be a lawyer, while the third was studying to be a business man. The fourth son worked for his father. The father even owned a store and his own home was almost completely paid for! They were a good family and worked very hard.

Their two daughters were intelligent, religious, and educated, but not very pretty. Josephine was married with two little children. She was a hairdresser and her husband beat her. Josephine, would never tell anyone. She knew that if she did she would shame her husband. Still she looked at her children carefully, every day to make sure they were not being hurt in any way.

Jennie was rather short and always wore long dresses and black tied shoes with little square heels. She was very clean and always smelled lovely like spring flowers. She had long, black hair, but she kept it rolled up in a bun at the back of her neck. She had a little gold clip in it, to keep it from tumbling down. She was named Jennie just as Na'am's older daughter was named.

They were married in Scranton in her family church, with all her brothers and her sisters surrounding her at every moment. Only mother and father went on the bus with Naaj. They did not have enough money for everyone, to go on the bus. Father had to use all the money which he had been saving, for a good and heavy winter coat for Mary Rose. The coat would have to wait.

Naaj was kind and polite to everyone and especially, to his own parents and Jennie's parents. He did not laugh or even smile once. Naaj looked tall and handsome in his church suit and starched white shirt. He had a new dark tie. No one could deny that he was the handsomest man in the room, along with Joseph. Jennie looked very elegant in her long, white, lace dress. She had her father and mother's wedding gift around her neck. It was a long lavaliere with a single large diamond, in the middle of it. She had a tiny diamond hanging daintily from each ear. She wore seven gold bangle bracelets on her arm. Her hair was done up in braids with little white flowers. It appeared like a crown high on her head. Josephine had done this for her sister with pride and joy in Jennie's glorious hair. Even though Jennie was not pretty she had dignity and smiled kindly, at everyone except Naaj. She was afraid to raise her eyes to his even once.

CHAPTER 2

The Family

Na'am sat by Jennie's mother. She had a large package wrapped, in heavy brown paper by her chair. Millie had given her some pink ribbon to tie around it. She had asked Mrs. Tabinski if she could buy some. It cost Millie ten cents. Mrs. Tabinski was generous with it unwinding an extra yard for Millie. Na'am gave the package to Mrs. Zaya, and asked that she open it later on when having supper with her family. It had seven loaves of freshly baked bread in it.

Mr. Zaya and Joseph went for a walk, by themselves. Mr. Zaya knew that Joseph was having a hard time. He had heard from his sons, at the university about Joseph's illness. He was anxious about helping Joseph, by offering gifts to go with his daughter. Joseph was a royal son. Joseph was doing Mr. Zaya's family a fine honor, by asking for his daughter. Still he gently offered Joseph many gold pieces as a dowry for his daughter. Joseph declined by thanking Mr. Zaya for his kindness. He said, "Your daughter does my house great honor. I know she comes from a good family; is pure and will always obey my son." Joseph's heart was heavy. He knew Na'am could use the money, but he was of a noble family, and it would be unseemly for him to accept. He had nothing to offer Mr.

Zaya's house either. However, he knew that accepting Mr. Zaya's daughter into his house, as his daughter-in-law was enough.

Na'am and Joseph had moved his bookcase and books to the attic. She had purchased a fine, tall lamp from Mr. Joe, for the three nickels and twelve pennies saved in the mason jar. Mr. Joe had paid four quarters for the lamp. Na'am added a whole loaf of freshly baked bread and a slice of her wonderful apple pie, to the purchase price and Mr. Joe couldn't have been more pleased. Na'am's jar of hand cream and old hairbrush went upstairs, too. The attic was freshly painted. It was clean and it was warm. The old bed had a thick quilt made with real goose feathers placed neatly on top. It had faded blue flowers on the print coverlet. Still it gave the room a comfortable feeling. They would be quite cozy up here. Perhaps Joseph would teach Na'am to read at last.

Na'am had been busy. She washed, ironed, and hung fresh, white curtains in their old, large, sunny bedroom. The big bed mattress hung out over the back porch railing to freshen it. It took all of them to do it. The bureau was polished until Mary Rose could see her sweet face in the old wood. Mary Rose cut almost all Na'am's flowers from her kitchen flower pots. She was careful to leave a few for Toffie's lapel on Saturday night. She washed an old glass carefully and put fresh water in it for the flowers. She placed the pretty bouquet on the lace doily, on top of the bureau.

Millie had purchased a sweet, little hat, with another of her precious quarters. It was made of brown straw, with little pink flowers all around the lace edge. She placed it beside Mary Rose's flowers on the bureau. Toffie bought a large box of mints each one wrapped, in colorful paper and boxed in tinfoil wrap. He placed it on the table by the window where the little clock stood ticking away. Soon they were done. The mattress was hauled in and the fresh sheets white as snow were placed on the bed. The pillows were fluffed and spotless covered with printed pillow cases. At the bottom of the bed was a quilt. Handmade squares from every bit of material, that had ever entered their home was worked into the quilt. It was colorful and heavy and lovely to look at. It would warm the newly married couple through the cold winters.

Na'am had left instructions for Mr. Joe. He was to purchase two legs of lamb and have them wrapped, in butcher's paper. He was to place them on the highest shelf, in the ice-box right under the ice. He was to purchase them one day, before their return from Scranton. Na'am had taken her gold wedding band to the pawn shop. It was pure gold. The man there had given her four dollars for it. She had thirty days to get it back. It would cost her five dollars to get it back. Na'am tucked two dollars in her shoe. She would not use those. She told Mr. Joe that he would find the first two dollars for the lamb meat, on the back porch, under the mat. She would also bake him a cherry pie. He had brought her cherries in a large box. The cherries were not so good on the bottom layer. Another quarter was used from the mason jar. She knew what to do with them and quickly set to work. All would be ready in order to bake and cook on their return. They would have a wonderful reception for Naaj and Jennie.

They would invite their parish priest to bless the wedding couple. They would invite Jennie's parents and family and they would invite all their friends and neighbors too. Na'am, Mary Rose, Millie, Joseph, and Toffie would work for three days, after work and well into the night preparing everything. They would be moving furniture and setting up a long table across the living room that was borrowed, from the funeral director, of their church. That was the first chore. Na'am took out a white, bed sheet from the closet, in the big bedroom, to use as a tablecloth. It hung over the long table almost to the floor. She would place a homemade cake in the center of it when she got back. Na'am then packed a small package of clothes for their overnight stay in Scranton. Joseph had a freshly ironed white shirt. She had a freshly ironed blouse, too. She would wear her long black skirt used only on Sunday. She packed their night clothes and underwear, with their tops. Na'am folded them down as small as possible and put them in a brown paper bag. She tied it neatly with a string. Then she had one more chore, before she went to bed. She set her dough to rise, for morning.

Naaj and Jennie were driving home, in a car, with Mr. and Mrs. Zaya. It was a wonderful car. Naaj had never ridden in one before. Jennie's sister Josephine and four brothers would come on the bus, with Josephine's two children. Her husband said he did not care to make the trip. He said he had to tend to other things.

They would be here soon. Na'am spent the last two quarters to buy extra rice. She made a huge pot of rice with spices and bits of the precious lamb meat in it. She had Toffie cut twelve clothes hangers in half and burn the paint off them all. Mary Rose washed and oiled them, with a bit of lamb fat. Millie and Na'am put chunks of lamb, with fresh onions and peppers, on the skewers. They were careful not to hold the ends carelessly, as they were sharp. Soon the skewers would be hard to handle as they seared and turned the meat till it was tender and sweet, over the hot coal stove. The flames shot up as the little bits of fat burned off the skewers. The two legs of lamb had been turned into twenty-four skewers of meat. Mr. Joe insisted Na'am take some lettuce and tomatoes as his gift to the bride and groom. He too, was invited to the party. Na'am graciously thanked him and turned them into a huge salad using her precious oil and a lemon for dressing.

Mr. Joe was worried about his clothes. He had two shirts and two pairs of pants, and an old sweater. One set was for work only and the other set was for church. He put on his clean church clothes. He had bought a gaily colored handkerchief and tied it under his chin as a necktie. He had only a torn, brown hat that kept his hair out of his eyes. Whenever he drove his horse and wagon up and down the streets he went hatless to Na'am's house. He was very neat and proper, with his hair parted, in the middle and slicked down.

Jennie sat alone in the big bedroom. She sat very still that even her eye lashes did not flutter. Na'am knocked gently on the door and entered. She went to Jennie and enfolded her in her arms. She understood what Jennie was feeling. She had felt the same way when after that first night, with her husband her own mother-in-law approached her, in the bedroom she had shared with Joseph. At last tears slipped down Jennie's face. Na'am held her close to her heart, for a long moment.

Then she looked at Jennie, standing there in her lace trimmed, white shift. Her legs were not normal. They extended out from the knees in a most strange position. So that was why she wore the long dresses and walked a bit to one side and then the other. It was not an ungraceful walk, but still not normal. Jennie had rickets as a baby. Mothers did not always have enough milk, for their children, in winter. They did not know the danger of this. It was why Na'am had given her children slices of cheese because there was little fresh milk, to be had. Even though her children would wrinkle their little noses up and sputter at the taste, she would make them take a little teaspoon of fish oil when she could get it because she knew it had value, in winter. They fought her and gagged, but Na'am fought them back and she won the battle every time. When Na'am was able she would give them figs, dates, and dried apricots, in the "old country." Here in America it was milk and cod liver oil. Sometimes she would find a few oranges and would give up something else that was needed, in order to get them. Her mother had told her that it was important.

Na'am said to Jennie, "It is not good to stay in here alone, all day. Naaj will be back tonight and we have much to do, before our men come home from work. Bathe yourself my daughter then dress and come down, to breakfast. We will talk while we work. It will be better for you to be busy." Little did she know that Jennie was not longing for Naaj to come home. She was dreading it. Naaj had not been kind and he did not love her. The only joy would be when she could produce a child; a son for him. She knew he did not love her. She knew it already, after only this first night that they had spent together.

Mary Rose was very cold, but she refused to wear her mother's old coat to school. Besides it was too small for her. Na'am made her wear a scarf and two long sweaters, Mary Rose's sweater and her own. She made her wear two pairs of stockings and they made her shoes too tight. Still she was very cold. Jennie was watching for her from her bedroom window which faced the front street. She looked at Mary Rose in surprise. "Come into my room little sister," she said, from the window. Mary Rose put her arms up to Jennie and she pulled her in through the window. They both laughed out loud, as Mary Rose fell into the arms of Jennie. "Where is your coat my little one? It's too cold for sweaters." Mary Rose lowered her eyes and said nothing. Jennie looked hard at Mary Rose. Suddenly she said, "Mary Rose let's go for a walk!" Jennie pulled her warm, black wool coat on. She had a bright kerchief to wear. It had been folded in her coat pocket.

They tip-toed down through the kitchen, and out the front door. Na'am was in the wash room ironing shirts and did not see them go out. Jennie headed toward the pawn shop. The dealer's eyes sparkled as he saw the pure gold bangle, that Jennie pulled off her arm. She was careful not to take more than one, from under her coat sleeve. "You must give me twenty-five dollars for this, she said. I know that it is twenty-four karat gold. My own father has told me so." The dealer replied back, "You will not tell me what I will give you. I will offer you twenty dollars and not a penny more," he said. Jennie did not answer him, but stared into his face. He wouldn't hold that bracelet for thirty days. He would sell it right away. He knew a gentleman who would give him forty dollars, for that kind of gold or maybe even fifty dollars, if he was sly enough.

Mary Rose was peering through the glass topped case. She had never been in the pawn shop before. Mary suddenly held her breath, "Wait! That is my mother's wedding ring there. I would know it anywhere? See Jennie! See! It is mother's ring." "Are you sure Mary Rose," asked Jennie? "Yes, Yes, it's true," she exclaimed. "Well sir, Jennie said calmly, I will take your twenty dollars for my bracelet however, I must have that ring thrown in, also."

"No! I know that lady. She will bring me seven dollars for her ring." Na'am had tried to buy time for her wedding band loan, by bringing the two dollars that she had hidden in her shoe because she had nothing left not even in the mason jar. The dealer had told Na'am that he would hold the ring another month however, she would have to pay him seven dollars more. Jennie turned to go. "Come Mary Rose, you must take me to another dealer." She pushed her bracelet back on her arm. Mary Rose hurried to the door. She wanted to stay longer and look at the beautiful things in the display cases, but the look on Jennie's face was not one she had seen before. "Now, now, let me show you another ring. I have many rings. Can't you pick another one out? The one you want is gold and very expensive." Jennie tossed her head and looked right into the dealer's eyes. "Twenty dollars and that gold ring!" "You are a very arrogant young lady. I should not do this however, for good business I will do it. Yes, you will see, I will do it."

Mary Rose looked at Jennie with admiration. "Jennie you are so strong-willed, how wonderful! I want to be just like you. To answer a man so; to get your price, to get mother's ring back! Oh Jennie, I love you. I am so glad you are my new sister." Jennie hugged Mary Rose and headed away from the dealer, in the opposite direction to their home. They stopped in front of another store, but this one was a little larger and had clothes in the window. "Jennie that is Mr. Keeler's store and everything in there is very expensive." "Come Mary Rose," and Jennie marched into the store. There were warm, pretty clothes everywhere and Jennie walked directly over to the coats. She pulled three of them off their hangers and told Mary Rose to try them on, one by one. She let her see herself in the long mirror. Mary Rose had never seen herself in a long mirror before. Suddenly, Mary Rose was overtaken with shame. "Oh Jennie, I cannot accept this from you. Father and mother would be so angry." "Mary Rose, there is a time for pride and there is a time for common sense. Don't you see, you will freeze or get sick or something. You must accept. Choose now, or else I will choose for you." They agreed on the navy blue, wool coat with the white buttons and tiny fur collar. It was the best and warmest coat Mary Rose had ever seen. It cost a whole ten dollars. Jennie paid it without a second thought. Mr. Keeler gave her two five dollar bills for her change. Jennie felt for the gold ring wrapped, in a bit of paper, in the bottom of her pocket. She wanted to keep it safe.

As soon as they got home, Jennie asked Na'am to come to her bedroom. Na'am could see something was going on and she saw the package Mary Rose was carrying somewhat behind her back. Na'am did not like this, it seemed something was very wrong. Jennie shut her bedroom door softly. Mary Rose went into the kitchen and sat down to wait. The package was placed under the table. She was fearful she would never get to wear it. Not a sound could be heard. The kitchen had an old clock. Mary Rose could hear it ticking loudly.

No-one else ever knew what was said. Na'am came out of Jennie's room with her face flushed red, and wiping her eyes with the back of her hand. Mary Rose looked at her mother's hand. Na'am was wearing her wedding ring once again. Jennie put one of the five dollar bills in the mason jar. Mary Rose and Na'am saw her do it, but said nothing. The other five dollar bill was smoothed out and placed on the table in the bedroom, by the little clock. It was the table Naaj used for his handkerchiefs and comb and other things he kept in his pockets. Jennie would explain everything to her husband that night. She must always be truthful with her husband. She would be. She planned to be a good wife to him no matter what. She had promised before God.

Na'am made a silent vow that she would pay Jennie back everything and more. She now loved this girl more than she loved herself because Na'am saw that she was kind and unselfish. She vowed she would not let her suffer in any way, if she could help it.

Two months had passed. Jennie was pregnant. Na'am knew, but no-one else. It was a happy time for Na'am. Jennie helped her everyday while the others were at work and school. Now Na'am would not let Jennie pick up the heavy laundry basket. She made her tea in the afternoon when most of the laundry was done and supper was simmering, on the stove. She would make Jennie sit in the old rocking chair and serve her tea, with lemon and sugar in it. She would give her a little fresh fruit and a slice of warm bread with cherry jam on it. Then Na'am would sit at the table, to have her own tea. Jennie would hug her little tummy even though no one could see any signs of her baby yet. She hoped to tell Naaj tonight, in their room. She cleaned his shoes wiping them to a nice shine and then she laid his fresh clothes out on the chair ready, for morning. She planned to brush out her long hair and then, before they went to sleep, she would whisper this lovely thing into his ear. Naaj was late tonight. Jennie said her prayers and fell asleep.

Toffie and Naaj came home smiling and laughing. They were happy tonight because they had received a small raise. It had been a great surprise. The company was pleased with all their workers who worked down, in the mines. The owners had made plenty of money this year no doubt about that. It was the first raise and the first recognition, of their good work. All their fellow workers were happy that night even though the raises were small. At least it was something more to bring home, to their families. Naaj planned to get his wife's bracelet out of the pawn shop, so he would save the little extra money, for now. After all she would likely give him a son one day. They had enjoyed two beers each, before coming home. It was just to celebrate, but on empty stomachs so, the beers went to Naaj's head. He didn't know that the bracelet had already been sold, at a nice profit for the dealer.

Toffie was going to take the whole family to the "Roxie" that Saturday night. He would pay for everyone. He would make his mother and father come along too. He would even make Millie come with them and pay for her ticket, too. She would not be able to flirt or even smoke in front of her parents. He told Millie he was going to treat them to ice cream afterwards. He knew Na'am would fuss at the expense and think it wasteful, but he would do it anyway. He could hardly wait to tell them.

How happy they were! What a pretty party they made! This family bound, in respect and love holding hands and laughing. All of them dressed, in their best church clothes finally, enjoying a little time together. Mary Rose proudly wore her new coat. Jennie had on the little straw hat with the lace and flowers around the edges, that Millie had so kindly put on her bureau. Millie wore her latest purchase. It was a little red hat made of felt, with gold piping on the brim. Mother and father sat together watching all the youngsters, on the dance floor, forgetting for a moment how hard life was. They counted their blessings and admired their own children. They had great joy in seeing them so happy. Na'am and Joseph held hands.

Jennie sat by Na'am watching too. She marveled at Mary-Rose's grace on the dance floor. Toffie was his usual happy self, always asking the little "wallflowers" to dance. He would not sit out any dance that night. He danced with Millie too. They were wonderful on the dance floor. Millie knew all the steps, as well as Toffie. They were doing steps no one had ever seen before. Everyone clapped for them when they finally finished exhausted and needing a drink of cold punch. Then Toffie made his mother dance with him surprised at how light she was, in his arms.

Naaj would not dance with Jennie. Her long dress covered her mis-shaped legs. He thought she could not dance and he was rather ashamed that she wasn't as pretty, as some of the other girls. Jennie could slow dance beautifully, but Toffie was afraid to ask her to dance until after Naaj did. After a long while everyone was astounded to see their father get up, from his chair next to their Mother and approach Jennie. He bowed to her and extended his hand out to her. Jennie smiled up at him and looked around for Naaj to see if she had his permission. He was nowhere to be seen. Jennie got up to dance with her father-in-law. It was a very sweet moment. All eyes were on this couple. Joseph was tall and handsome. He had elegant bearing. He took each of Jennie's hands in his and danced her around the room. They were in perfect step with each other. Then Joseph twirled Jennie around and they began to laugh looking at each other, and enjoying the moment. They did not miss a step.

Toffie glanced up suddenly, as he spotted Geraldine Walena's bright, flowing, blond hair outside the side window. She was running with Naaj and he had his arm around her. At that moment Millie looked up too, then startled, she looked at Toffie. Millie slipped out the side door. She ran after Naaj and Geraldine, but they seemed to be no longer there.

Joseph and Jennie finished dancing and Joseph brought the smiling girl back to her chair. He glanced at Toffie and Millie. Millie looked frightened. Joseph went towards the door. He said it was to catch his breath. There he saw in the moonlight Naaj and Geraldine, in the small of a large tree. They were in an embrace.

They all went directly home. The ice cream treat was forgotten. All their happiness gone, as they walked away from the music. Joseph made Naaj go up to Joseph's attic room. They heard the door slam shut and the click of the lock was very loud, to those below in the kitchen. They could only hear the sound of shouting, not the words except, for one or two phrases that no walls could hide. "Shame to my house!" It was Joseph's voice. Naaj's voice was tense and loud, "Ugly woman!" It was heard clearly! Now Na'am rose up and left the kitchen, without a word. Mary and Millie went to their room, both were silent. Jennie and Toffie sat alone at the kitchen table. Toffie touched Jennie's hand gently. Her face was like stone. Her little straw hat had fallen, to the floor.

Naaj had been gone from his home for three days, but showed up at work everyday looking like a ghost. Jennie had not spoken to anyone. If it were not for the child she was carrying she would have returned, to her father. She would have left the same night, but she had vowed before God and man, in church to be a good and faithful wife. She did not take her vows lightly. Now she had a little one to think about. She knew she would have a much better life, with her own family in Scranton where she knew she was loved. Where there was always too much to eat and where she had no worries or slights to bear. She thought long and hard about this. She would stay here, for now, for the sake of her baby.

Naaj finally dragged himself home. His face was gaunt. He had nowhere else to go. He went into the bathroom to bathe. When he came out he told his Mother that he was very sorry and ashamed. He planned, in truth, to beg Jennie's forgiveness. He went to their bedroom, to face Jennie. He lay down to rest a moment until Jennie would come in. She was in the kitchen not sure what to do. Jennie made up her mind to face her husband and knocked lightly, at the door. There was no answer. She entered to find Naaj sprawled, on the bed and burning with fever. He had a strange red color to his face. He did not seem to know her. Jennie called Na'am to the door. "Mother I think there is something very wrong. Do not enter. Please go for the doctor right away, please mother do as I ask, I beg you." Jennie locked the door until the doctor would come. She had seen this thing before, as a child, in the "old country." Na'am did as she asked. She ran to the doctor's house, without her old coat, and even without her hat. When she returned she went to the mason jar to get the five dollars, that would be needed for the doctor and the medicine that might be needed. Then she sat down overcome with fear.

Naaj had Smallpox! The county sent a man to put a sign on their front door that said in large red letters, "Quarantined" and instructions that no one was, to enter or leave the house. Joseph, Millie, Toffie, and Mary-Rose had nowhere to go. Na'am shouted through the front door to Joseph, "My husband please, please, go to Mr. Joe's house. Tell him I will settle with him later and remember to thank him from your hearts. Be grateful, for he is a kind man," she said. She knew that Mr. Joe would not refuse them no matter how crowded it would be.

Mr. Joe gave Joseph and Mary Rose his own bed. Millie slept on his funny, old couch. Toffie and Mr. Joe slept, on the floor. He was flattered and honored that they came to him. Mr. Joe shared his supper of stew with them. It was a bit thin, but he made it go around taking much less for himself. Millie and Mary washed the dishes and sat down to pray. Then Mary took out her school books to study. She spread her things out on Mr. Joe's kitchen table. Mr. Joe had a radio in his other room. He asked Joseph if he could turn it on. Mr. Joe was very polite and rather, in awe of this gentleman. Millie and Toffie asked Mr. Joe if they could listen, to the radio too. Later Mary lay down by her father and pulled the cover over his shoulders. It was cold. Mary missed her Mother and her own warm, sweet bed. They had to sleep in their clothes.

Mr. Joe rose early in the morning, to go to work. First, he put on a large pot of oatmeal to cook, for their breakfast. He packed lunches of fruit and biscuits in brown sacks, for each of them. It was all he had for now. Tonight he would bring much more to his little house. He would go into the market and bring everything he could carry. During the day he went to the back door, of Na'am's house. She had a package for each of them, with fresh, clean clothes in them. She thanked Mr. Joe for everything. He told her not to talk of money. He was lonely and this was very comforting, to him to finally have voices, in his house, especially, these voices. He asked if they were all well. He asked for messages he could carry, from Na'am to her family. Then when the door closed he left a box of apples, good apples, on the back porch, where she could see them, from the laundry room.

CHAPTER 3

Losses

J ennie sat in the chair beside her husband who lay, in a
restless sleep. She was exhausted. She had not left
their bedroom for two weeks, except to use the bathroom.
She felt so dirty and needed to bathe, but was afraid to
leave him. She carried the buckets of waste and the soapy
water and rags she had used, to wash Naaj on a daily basis,
out to the back yard. She dug a deep hole and threw the
waste and rags into it. She poured salt over it all and
covered the spot, with dirt again. The fever had broken, but
Naaj's handsome face and body had horrible, dry scabs all
over it. He wasn't throwing up any more. He was taking
some water to drink now. Everyday, she would try to feed
him some hot soup. Na'am made it fresh daily for them. It
was made from mostly vegetables, but sometimes there was
a little handful of rice thrown, into the pot as well. She
would leave it on a flat board, with her fresh bread, on a
little table outside their bedroom door.

Na'am was tired too. She had never been this tired.
She thanked God everyday, for Jennie. She thanked God
everyday that she had not spent Jennie's five dollars so that
she was able to pay the doctor and buy the medicine, for
Naaj. There was a dollar left, but she was afraid to spend it.

She thanked God for everything and begged him to keep safe the baby that Jennie carried deep, within her. She scrubbed every bit of the house, with hot water containing salt. She opened all the windows and the back door, to let the fresh air flow through. She boiled water to pour over the soup bowls, spoons, and even the water glasses, after she had washed them in hot, soapy water. Her hands were rough and raw. She was too tired to climb up to the attic each night, so she slept in the living room, on the couch.

Jennie would not let her into the bedroom to see Naaj. The doctor was very happy that he had been able to save this young man. He was astounded, at these women, who were so careful about their family members, by sending them away. Still they gave him such care even, at a distance. The care given to Naaj was better than at the hospital. If only his other patients were so carefully cared for he would have been able to save a few more of them. The disease was so contagious. Mothers did not know how to keep their little ones safe. Some recovered and some did not.

Na'am knocked on the door, but she heard soft voices. Na'am tip-toed away. Naaj was awake. He whispered to Jennie that he was sorry, and very ashamed. He was telling her he would do anything to thank her and knew that he would grow, to love her very much, if she would allow him to. Jennie sat on the edge of the bed and put her arms around him.

When he was asleep again, she sat on the chair to rest a little. Soon she was asleep too. She did not see the blood pouring down, from under her long dress, to soak the rug beneath the chair.

Now Na'am was taking care of both of them. Her heart was heavy. Jennie was very pale. Na'am took the crucifix down, from the living room wall. She carried it to

Mary and Millie's bedroom. She placed it on the table where Jennie could see it from their bed.

The doctor said that Naaj could return to work, in another week. He would have to go back to the mines, because they were very late with the mortgage payment. He was pock-marked on his face and body. His handsome face was ruined forever. But, he was returning to good health. Na'am helped him into the living room so she could change his bed. Those sheets and rags used to wash him were buried, in the corner of the yard too. The bedroom was scrubbed down and all the windows were left open. The county came to take down the quarantine sign, with the big red letters.

Jennie awoke. She stared at the crucifix! She felt so empty. Her stomach was very flat. The doctor said she would never be able to have a baby. Not ever! He had worked hard to save her life, but she didn't want her life anymore. Na'am came in to her. She dragged the old rocking chair over to the bed. Then she brought soup, hot and filling and tried to feed Jennie. Jennie turned her face away. Na'am stood up, exhaustion had drained her face of all beauty. She was angry now. Jennie, you are my daughter now! I make a promise to you, God will not abandon you. God will give you children, lots of children! It is a holy desire! So, I promise this, my child. But, you must believe and you must have faith in the good Lord. Jennie turned her face away from the crucifix, and Na'am. She faced the wall.

The family was home! Mary flung the front door open and was enveloped, in her mother's arms. Mary danced her around in twirls. "Mind now, my child!" Na'am was smiling at them all. Joseph hugged his wife and kissed her cheeks again and again. Toffie and Millie hugged their mother and kissed her, without stopping. Na'am laughed and hugged them back. Mr. Joe was carrying their washed clothes in a bushel basket. He set it down on the kitchen floor. He could smell that wonderful bread baking in the oven! Na'am went over to Mr. Joe. She said, "Mr. Joe you are welcome in this house always! Every Sunday you must come over for Sunday dinner, with the whole family. We will not take no for an answer and tonight you will be our guest of honor."

Mary Rose had been off from school for ten days, and went back only yesterday. Even the schools had been closed. She had kept busy studying and then cleaned Mr. Joe's house. She made suppers and even hung curtains up, as best she could. She had found them, at the second hand store, for only a few pennies. She washed, mended, and ironed them. They had big yellow flowers splashed on them. When she hung them up they made the whole kitchen look different. Millie had washed the kitchen floor, before they left Mr. Joe's house. She had baked a tray of potatoes and onions, with slices of a sausage. It smelled so good. Later she wrapped the food in some butcher paper, and placed it under the ice, on the topmost shelf. Mr. Joe would have his supper all ready for tomorrow night.

Mary Rose could not wait to see Jennie. She ran around looking for her. Her bedroom door was closed. Mary banged on it! "Jennie, Jennie I have something very important to tell you. You will be so happy! You will not believe it!" Jennie opened her door. She flung her arms around Mary Rose. She sobbed, "I missed you so! My dear little sister, I missed you so!" Millie and Toffie and Joseph crowded around her. Telling her they missed her and they loved her. They could see she had suffered. She was so thin now. Mary found her hairbrush and brushed Jennie's hair until it shone again. She piled her hair up on her head, in a roll and put Jennie's little gold hair clip in it. There!

That is very pretty Jennie. You look more like my old Jennie again.

Na'am had set the table. She had pulled an old box over and put a cushion on it, for herself. Toffie went to get Naaj. He wanted to make sure he was steady on his feet. They clasped shoulders and they smiled, at each other. Toffie winked at Jennie. They all smiled. Mr. Joe turned to leave. "No! No! We will not let you go Mr. Joe! Mother has made an extra seat for you." They all laughed again. Mother brought the loaves of hot bread to the table. She had made a huge kettle of soup and she had rice, with string beans and a few pine nuts in it. For dessert she had apple pie. She had hoped to make a cake, but perhaps another time.

They were all so excited that they had not noticed there, on the front porch was a little sack of peaches, a plate with homemade cookies that were still warm, some yellow snap dragons, a large bag of fresh greens and field flowers, in an old jar. The neighbors and friends all around them were happy, to see the sign taken off the front door, and their children and family reunited again. They remembered all the small gestures of kindness that Na'am had shown them through the years.

Mary Rose was so excited while telling her family about her surprise. Something had happened today at school! She said that Sister Lucia, who usually came to ask for pennies, for the missions had brought a gentleman, from St. Michael's Church, across town, to visit their school. All the students were brought to the auditorium to listen to him speak. He said because of the sickness there were many children, with no parents. There were babies, young children, and even teenagers, with no place to go. There were twenty-three children who needed homes. Many were hoping to be adopted. Some of the children were brothers and sisters. The older ones could work in homes or farms for their keep. They asked the children to tell their parents there would be a meeting at school very soon and people should come, to see the children. Jennie looked at Mary Rose. Tears silently fell from her eyes. She quickly brushed them away. She would not spoil the family dinner.

CHAPTER 4

Mary Rose Gains a New Sister

T he family was ready to go, to the meeting. They had missed each other dearly, so all of them decided to go. Mary's "surprise" had hurt Jennie deeply. Mary was too young and inexperienced to realize that this was not the same as holding her own dear, little baby in her arms. But her innocence had opened this door. Jennie wouldn't even consider another child. It was too soon to think of all this. She would go to please Mary. She would not take home any child. Jennie had made up her mind!

Mr. Joe had asked to go with them. He could use some help. Perhaps an older boy, who would like to brush down his horse, or to keep him company on his rounds. He would treat him kindly and even pay him a little. He was very lonely now that their family had left his little house.

He had enjoyed watching Millie as she had worked, in his kitchen. He missed her presence very much. She was so direct. She was "no-nonsense" about everything. Yet, she looked sweet in her little hat and was very soft spoken most of the time. He knew that she was way above him, in education and breeding. He realized that she was a real lady used to gentleness and kindness. He also knew their family had always been on the edge of poverty, even though they never said so. They always seemed to meet their many obligations, but were just a breath away from absolute need. On his rounds he had seen many families fall apart or move away. It was always the same and very sad to see. They were poor except, for the families who lived on the big hill. Yet, he might speak to Joseph. He felt he already knew the answer would be no!

The little boy held onto Naaj's leg. He would not let go. Each one in the family tried to pick him up; tried to catch his attention, tried to hug him. But this little blue-eyed child would not let go of Naaj's leg. Finally, Naaj picked him up way over his head. His fine brown, baby hair falling over his forehead. They laughed at each other. The little boy looked right into Naaj's eyes. He didn't seem to mind all the pock marks, in Naaj's face. In fact, he didn't seem to even see them. He snuggled in Naaj's lap and promptly went to sleep. Jennie turned away. She had a stern look in her eyes.

They walked home together softly chatting about all the children they had seen. When they were almost home they saw that there was a car, in front of their house. "Father, Father" Jennie cried out! She out-ran all of them. She went right into her Father's arms, but his face was very sad. He couldn't hide it, though, he tried. He was glad to see his daughter, but he had sad news and he had come to bring her home, to Scranton. Her mother was nearly out of her mind with grief!

Josephine and her husband had taken the children on a little drive, in the country. She was happy about it and thought it might be a good way for them, to spend time together alone, as a little family. Her husband had started drinking before they left the house. Then he pulled out a flask from under the dashboard and took steady drinks, as he drove along. Josephine did not want to ride with him

46

anymore. She cried until she got him to stop the car. She took the children out of the back seat and they began to walk. Her husband got more angry at every step they took. Josephine would not argue with him over this. He stopped the slowly, moving car and dragged her to the front seat. He pushed her into the car. He struck her several times. "Children, you must run. Barbara, run as fast as you can with Philip. Obey me...!" she cried. Little Barbara ran. She dragged her baby brother Philip down a steep incline and they tumbled over and over. They hid under a little bush and were very quiet. They were very frightened.

Josephine's face was bruised and she had a cut, on her cheek, from the heavy ring her husband wore. He started the car pressing his foot, on the gas as hard as he could and it lurched ahead out of control. He hit a huge tree not a quarter of a mile away. The farmer standing there, in his field saw it all. At first, he didn't know what to do. Then he heard children crying, somewhere. He came out of his shock and ran to the car! It was very quiet, except for the sound of the motor which was still running. Neither the man nor the woman moved. There was blood everywhere. They lay in twisted positions. He screamed to his wife. He ran down the hill following the sound, of the crying children.

Jennie was gone! She left with her father the next morning. Na'am had risen early, to pack them some biscuits and jam. She put strong, hot coffee in two jars that had lids. She remembered to put a spoon and knife, into the paper sack. The house was silent. Na'am thought, Lord, Is there no end to our sorrow? She prayed for their safe journey. She prayed and trusted God.

Naaj was very lonely. He missed Jennie more than he ever thought possible. He missed her kindness and her gentle smile. He would come home every night thinking surely, she would have come home. It had been months. Perhaps she was not coming home ever again.

He had been visiting the little boy every Sunday, after breakfast. He begged Sister Lucia not to let anyone else adopt him. The little boy ran to Naaj every time. He hugged his legs and would not let him go. Naaj always brought him a little present.

A green, wooden truck just big enough for his little hand was his favorite gift, from Naaj. An oatmeal cookie from his mother's kitchen was eaten, in a moment. Naaj bought a second hand, wooden crib and took the large package, into their bedroom, It was still in pieces. He propped it up in the closet. He would put it together, with nails and paint it, if Jennie would only say so. He took something wrapped in a piece of white paper out, of his pocket. He placed it carefully on the lace doily on Jennie's bureau.

He had gone to the pawn broker and told him to buy Jennie's bracelet back. He would pay double to get it back. The dealer wasn't sure how to do this. He had sold it the very day the girls had come, into his shop. Naaj picked the dealer up with one hand and held him against the wall. "I will pay you double. Buy it back and I will be here next week to get it!" The dealer said, "Yes Sir!" I will do it, you will see, I will do it!" He hoped he could.

He would tell the gentleman, on the hill that he had made a mistake and offer him some gold pieces in its place. The gentleman didn't care. He was only interested in gold. The dealer smiled. They would both make a profit.

Still Jennie had not come back. The time went by slowly for them all.

CHAPTER 5

Na'am Gains Her Independence

N a'am was feeling a little less tired this morning. She missed her little daughter-in-law very much. She went into Jennie's bedroom and sat by the window, in the old rocking chair. She watched the school children, as they walked by, on both sides of the street. The little ones were in small groups laughing and skipping and pushing each other their coats open, to the warming sun. Across the street, going the other way were the older children, some in uniforms of white shirts and blue pants or skirts. They were all carrying books and some had lunch pails. The sun felt good on her head and face. She propped her head up on both hands, while leaning her elbows, on the window sill.

She thought about her reading lessons. Almost every night Joseph would teach her, after they got into their old bed. She would sit up straight, with a pencil and a book, of lined school paper on her lap. Joseph had given her his own notebook and she would do her abc's for him. Now she was writing words and even reading a little here and there from his newspaper! She had found an old, child's, picture book, at the second hand store. The woman there gave it to her. Joseph laughed at his little wife when he saw it but he taught her the words. She saw that it was a child's story, but she liked reading it out loud to Joseph. She was so pleased with their little secret. He was happy that she could learn so quickly. Whenever he looked at her he was seeing her, as he always did, for that first time standing in her father's field. Her beautiful, dark hair tumbling out of her hat and curling around her fresh, sun-tanned face. Her bare arms were round and smooth the color of apricots. He never failed to see her in just that way. Although now they were both gray haired and had lines, of worry forever creased, in each gentle face.

Na'am noticed a child walking behind the others. She was rather thin. She had a sweater on instead of a coat, and she had no scarf. She had a little book, but no lunch sack. She called to the child. "Little one, I have two biscuits, with jam on it left from breakfast, would you be so kind as to eat them for me? I am ashamed to throw them away. It would be such a waste." The little girl looked up at the lady, in the window not sure of what she was hearing. "Thank you ma'am, I will eat them." The child's hands almost shook when Na'am handed them carefully, from the window down to her. Then Na'am said, "Thank you my child."

Na'am hurried to the grocery store. She had an idea. She asked the grocery man if she could buy a box of licorice and a box of long pretzels. It cost two dollars. They were going to be late with the mortgage again, anyway. Naaj had kept his raise money and had given her one dollar less than usual, for weeks. The bank manager did not say anything yet, but she knew he would very soon.

Na'am nailed the small board she used as a tray to the outside of the window sill. She opened the box of candy and the box of pretzels. She put a little soup dish in the window sill. Then she got her notebook and tore out a page. She made a little sign. It said, "One Penny Each." Then she went indoors to start Mrs. Janeski's wash. She was very late. She must remember to hide everything before the family came home.

Mr. Joe wanted to talk with Joseph privately. He could no longer think of Millie walking out or dancing with another man. She was young and pretty and soon, very soon, without any doubt, he knew someone would come calling at her door.

If Joseph said "no" to Mr. Joe then he would not trouble this house again. He just had to know if he could ask Millie out. He knew now he wanted her for his wife.

He had taken a young man into his home. He was from that orphan home, that Sister Lucia talked about. He was a great help to Mr. Joe. He could work longer hours because the boy would sweep his house and start a stew for supper. Mr. Joe taught him how to do all this. Sometimes he even brought a sausage home for a treat especially, if he had a loaf of Na'am's bread to go with it. The young man would carry their wash to the old neighbor lady, who was glad to do it all, for a dollar a week. He would talk with Mr. Joe as they brushed down, feed, and water Betsy, his horse and old friend. Then they would go in to supper.

Mr. Joe made Jerry go to school and do all his homework faithfully. He was sixteen years old. He bought him a warm pair of pants and a school shirt. He bought him another pair of pants and a white shirt for church. He even bought him a warm coat. He paid him a dollar every week. The young man was so grateful, that at first he refused the money. Mr. Joe said he would save it for him every week, for whenever he wanted it, or whenever he wanted to leave him. He would keep his word. Mr. Joe was able to go to the next town to peddle his fruits and vegetables too. Because of the boy's help, he made more money and shared it. But mostly he saved it, lots of it, through the years.

Joseph thought Mr. Joe was a good and kind man and it was time to be an "American gentleman" himself. It didn't matter that he was of royal lineage here in America. He said, "Mr. Joe, you have proven yourself many times, so you may ask Millie herself, if she will walk out with you." Mr. Joe was very happy, but now he was scared. How did I dare to ask this he thought. Still he was overjoyed.

It was late, and Na'am hurried to the window to take everything inside. She wanted to hide it all before her family came home. The little dish was full of pennies. The box of pretzels was almost empty. The candy was half gone. Na'am could not believe it! She put all the pennies into the mason jar. It was half full. There was even a nickel in there too.

The next morning she put out the candy and the few pretzels that were left. She wanted to watch for the little girl. Perhaps she would accept another biscuit or a slice of bread. She came again and looked up at the window. Hope beamed through her blue eyes. Na'am ran to get her the slice of bread. Right behind her was a little boy. He held up a penny, but he did not want candy. He wanted a slice of bread with a smudge of jam on it. He looked well cared for, so she took his penny with a smile. So it went. Now she was making more and more bread. The children wanted a biscuit or a slice of her bread. Very few children wanted the candy. Na'am would cut the thick slices with joy. She began to make hot cookies, too. She had to get a wash pail to hold all the pennies. Now and then a woman would come along and ask for a whole loaf of bread. She would pay a whole quarter for it. Sometimes a man would come to ask for some biscuits, too.

After two weeks had gone by Na'am went to the grocery store. She bought a large sack of flour. She needed new yeast too. As she was leaving she thought she would spend a nickel for three apricots. It would be a lovely treat.

The grocer asked her if she had made the bread his little son had let him taste. He asked if she would bake seven loaves every week, for his store. Na'am said she would make him a loaf for free. She would think about his offer. She didn't know if she could keep up, with all the extra work. She would try.

The next day, as soon as everyone left the house and she had set up her window sill, being careful to wrap the slices of bread in her precious school paper Na'am put on her church dress and hat. She picked up the heavy bucket of pennies and nickels. She took her mortgage money and folded it into her pocket. She walked slowly to the bank. The bucket was very heavy. She asked for the mortgage man.

Joseph usually brought the house payment in himself. "Yes, Mrs. may I help you?" "I am Joseph's wife. I have come to pay the mortgage today." The manager looked over the top of his glasses. He invited her to sit down by his desk. He looked at the bills that she handed him. I am sorry Mrs., but you are short by fifteen dollars. "Oh No Sir I am not. It is right here." The man glanced down at the bucket of pennies and nickels. How do you know how much is in there, he asked. She replied, "Because I have counted them." "Oh!" said the manager. "Thank you just leave them on my desk I guess," not sure what else to say. "No sir, you must give me a paper that says I have paid the mortgage this month." The manager smiled, and asked "Can you read it even if I give it to you?" Many other people could not, of course. "Yes, sir, I can," said Na'am, just a little proud. So the manager gave a loud sigh. He could see he would have to accept the pennies and nickels. It was money after all. He could see he would have to stay late to count it all. He wrote out a receipt, and gave it to Na'am. She carefully folded it and put it way down deep in her pocket. She hurried home to start her work. She was going to make a large stew and an apricot cake. She had set her dough to rise, and hoped the family would not notice the amount. Tomorrow she would take seven loaves, no, eight loves to the grocery. Na'am had another new idea.

CHAPTER 6

Naaj Grows into Manhood at Last

Na'am called to the little girl, her first little friend. "Sweet child, where do you live?" The child pointed down the street, towards the house with the broken fence. "What is your papa's name?" The child's eyes filled with tears, and she put her head down. Na'am asked, "What is your mama's name?" "Loretta," replied the little girl. "Thank you," said Na'am, and "What is your name my little one?" "My mama calls me sweetheart, but I am Lora." Na'am moved the bowl of pennies to one side. "Ah yes! Now come here for your cup of milk, and a warm biscuit. See I have some cookies for you to take to school today."

Little Sweetheart had answered her questions, without knowing it. Her papa must have died with the smallpox sickness, and her mama was hard pressed to keep them both fed and warmly clad, that she could see. Na'am knew well the hardships of poverty. She would walk to Loretta's house soon, to ask her if she would come to work in her kitchen, and help her to keep up with her work. She would pay her as well as she could.

All of a sudden she missed her own mother's warm and clean kitchen, of long ago. There was always something good to eat, but she knew it must all be no more. She wondered, as always, if any of her family was left. Sometimes while gazing at the crucifix, she would try to remember something else, hanging up beside it, from long ago. Not in her mother's house, but in her grandmother's cottage. But, she could not quite remember what it was.

Something was changing inside Na'am's mind. Life would be different for her children if she could help it. Why not, wasn't this place called the "land of the free?" She remembered that huge statue in New York Harbor. She could not read what it said, but, she clearly remembered the cheers on board their ship when they first sighted it, even while the ship was far off. And something else, it was a statue of a woman! She did not understand that then, but she did now.

She would ask that little child's mother Loretta, to come now. Na'am could no longer keep up with everything anyway and still hide things before the family got home. She would gladly pay her for her work. She thought Lora's mother might be glad of it, too. She changed her mind, she would not wait. She took off her apron and put on her black church hat!

The grocer told Na'am that a servant from up the hill, who came to do the shopping for an employer that lived up there, had bought a loaf of Na'am's bread. Now she must make seven loaves every day! And he would take anything else she could bake! Na'am needed even more help. Summer was coming and Mary would be home from school. She too had to help in the kitchen.

She must tell Joseph! She would do so, that night. Na'am was afraid. Perhaps Joseph would be ashamed of her or offended by what she was doing. She must ask Joseph for another special thing too. She had saved enough for a very small down payment on a truck. If Joseph thought it wise they would tell Naaj to buy it, but they must go to the bank manager, for the loan. She could help with the payments now.

The men would do it soon she thought. Naaj and Toffee could haul the coal rather than go down into the mines. Na'am hated the mines even more than Naaj did. No day went by that she did not have fear in her heart for all the men in the mines, but especially, for her sons. She would watch the hills surrounding the mines and some of them had fires underground sending the smoke up, into the air day and night. She prayed harder before her mother's holy crucifix. Naaj must go to Scranton to beg Jennie to come home, before it was too late. She knew his heart was heavy and that he missed her very much. He would have already gone to her. He feared she would loath his face or remember that she had lost their baby because of him. Na'am knew he longed for Jennie. He must find out if she would come back to him. Na'am would see to it very soon.

She had sewn a mattress cover with her neat stitches and then filled it with a couple of soft, old, and worn blankets. She was sure to make it firm. It fit the crib snuggly. Na'am had found the brown crib pieces in the closet when putting the laundry away. She asked Mr. Joe to put it together, whenever he had a few extra minutes he tried to fix it. Naaj laughed when he saw his efforts. He set to work himself, making it straight and strong. Mary washed down the old wood and waxed it with a little sweet oil, from Na'am's medicine box. She had used it before, warmed on the old stove, just for earaches in the winter.

Millie made little printed sheets from a larger one. Then she purchased some soft blue yarn from Mrs.

Janeski. It took some of Millie's hidden quarters, but she didn't mind at all. Millie crocheted a beautiful, blue blanket of soft wool. Her mother corrected a stitch or two. She had taught Millie and Mary what her own Mother had taught her. Millie was humming to herself as she rocked and worked. She liked Mr. Joe very much. She wished he would kiss her, but he did not, at least not yet. She would be happy to be his wife and fix up his house and even have his babies. She marveled at how slow he was at asking her out. Still he had managed to get her father's permission. She was very happy that he had that kind of courage. Soon she thought, soon. So far they had gone for long walks. It was a good beginning.

They all left the church together. Na'am glowed with happiness. Her family had all come with her to Confession and Holy Communion. She turned in the opposite direction of their home. "Where are you going mother?" Mary Rose hurried after her mother. They were all looking forward to their breakfast after mass. "We are going to the bus station today. Naaj is going to Scranton to get Jennie and bring her home."

Naaj looked at his mother and father astounded. Na'am handed him his change of clean clothes packaged in a brown paper bag and neatly tied with string. "Give this other little package to Jennie from me, my son." He could smell the delicious, fresh bread through the brown paper. Joseph handed Naaj the bus ticket. There were some dollar bills in the envelope too. Na'am gave him a small paper sack with a few boiled eggs and some biscuits, for his breakfast on the bus. Father had given him enough money for two return tickets. The he pressed a little extra money into his hand too. "Son, buy some flowers for Jennie."
Naaj replied, "What of work father, we must not miss the mortgage payment." "Don't worry son, Toffie and I are

58

going to see the bank manager tomorrow." "All will be well, God's blessings my son." Na'am hugged her son. They all did. Then they began to turn back towards their home. Toffie gave Naaj a push in the opposite direction, and laughed. Naaj stood there watching them all. He waved good-bye to them, with a huge smile on his face. He turned and with new determination he walked swiftly towards the bus station.

Toffie spent every evening polishing their truck. It was dark blue and not too new, but sturdy and big. He painted the words "Brothers Coal Haul" on both doors. He had gone to see the mine owners to ask, for the job of hauling coal. These two brothers had done a good job while working in the mines. They didn't know how to do anything but work hard. The mine owners knew of Joseph and his fine reputation. They had all had a taste of Na'am's bread from time to time, throughout the years. They told Toffie that he and his brother could start after a week, on a Monday morning. They could haul coal for them everyday and for as long as they wanted.

There was a knock on the front door. How strange! Everyone knew that Na'am never locked her door to anyone. The family was at supper and all of them were tired. They had worked hard that day as usual. No matter, everyone was welcome in their home.

Toffie opened the door. He stared and then called his father and mother. There was Naaj! And there was Jennie! "Ah! At last, cried their mother. At last my children are home again!" She hugged Jennie tight, but then she froze. What was she seeing! Hiding behind her son and daughter-in-law were two little children. There was a small girl with big, dark eyes and a little boy, with bright, smiling eyes. "Mother, said Jennie, before I enter your home I must ask if my sister Josephine's children might enter with me.

They must go where I go, for they are mine now." Na'am said, "My dear one, you must ask your father-in-law and your husband, because you already know my answer." Jennie put her arms around Na'am and held her gently. She whispered to her "Thank you mother, thank you."

Joseph and Toffie clapped Naaj on his back and shook his hand and embraced him. Mary Rose and Millie each scooped up a child. They sat them on their laps and warmed their little, cold hands, and fed them from their own plates. Na'am ran to get more plates and glasses; she poured milk for them all. Coffee was perking on the old stove. It smelled so good!

"Mother what has happened around here?" Jennie came into the kitchen early, in the morning. She was rolling up her sleeves and putting on an old white apron. She had purpose in her step now. She had children to take care of. She and Naaj were happy together, more than they thought could be possible and happy to be in their own bed again. The little ones slept in Mary Rose and Millie's bed. They must buy two little beds from the second hand store.

Jennie found the gold bracelet on her bureau and she tenderly kissed Naaj's pit marked face. She no longer noticed the scars. She saw the baby crib filled with the pretty things each one had made. She never felt so loved before, as she did today. She knew she belonged in this house and in this family.

She poured the fresh hot coffee into cups for them both and as they drank it they worked and talked. She glanced up at Na'am's face with pride, after she heard all that had happened. "Mother, I will help you. We will do even more together. But you must not do the wash for Mrs. Janeski, it is far too much for you. You must make the wonderful bread, cakes, cookies, and biscuits. You must save your strength, to do the things that God has given you to do." Na'am knew that Jennie was right. She could not do it all.

Loretta was glad of the extra money. She agreed to do the wash at her house from this very week, however, Mrs. Janeski said that Na'am must teach Loretta how to starch and iron her husband's shirts, exactly as she likes them. She was very fussy.

Little Sweetheart was looking so much better these days. She smiled and skipped up and down the sidewalk, playing hopscotch. Her little cheeks were filling out and were quite pink. Her mother bought her a warm, second hand coat. It was a little long for her. Her mother said by fall it would fit her child, and be just right for school. She planned to buy her a brand new pair of shoes too, even though she had pieces of cardboard in her own.

Jerry had come by to fix her fence and repair a window. He even promised to fix a broken step in her basement. Loretta offered him a cup of coffee. He would have helped her even more however, he had to go to work with Mr. Joe.

Mr. Joe didn't mind waiting the extra hour. He lingered in Na'am's kitchen whenever he could. He wanted to watch Millie get ready for work; combing her lovely hair and rolling it up in a bun, at the back of her neck. Then he would drink coffee with her. Millie would pack bread and jam for him and Jerry too. A little later Mr. Joe would walk her to work. Now and then he stole a kiss from her. Millie thought, "Now that is more like it" and she thought his kisses very sweet.

Naaj and Jennie went to Sister Lucia that very Sunday. "How soon can we come for little Joey?" they asked. Sister Lucia looked intently at Jennie. "You may take him with you right now! He has waited long enough for you." Naaj thanked Sister Lucia profusely. Sister smiled at him. She knew they would be good to little Joey. She had grown fond of the little one herself. Naaj signed a paper in the office. Joey put his little hand into Jennie's and held tightly to it.

So as easily as that, he went out the door riding on Naaj's tall shoulders, but clinging to Jennie's warm hand. He walked into Na'am's house, as if he knew it was his house. When Naaj put him on his little feet he fell down on his sturdy behind, but it was to Na'am that he reached for a hug. That was that; he was home. He began to play with his little green truck under the kitchen table. Barbara and Philip went under the table too. Jennie laughed out loud for the first time, it was a wonderful sound. She was becoming happy again. She was even losing her shy ways, as she became a mother once again. It was then that she remembered Na'am's promise that morning when she saw, from the bed the old brown, carved crucifix propped up on the table, in Mary and Millie's room.

Millie and Mr. Joe were married that summer. The church where they went to mass each Sunday, with all the family had all the candles lit. Father Williams was smiling. These were good people, he thought. Millie was very beautiful in her new, white, lace dress, and her new, matching bonnet. Mrs. Janeski said the bonnet was her wedding gift to Millie. She begged her not to leave her employment. She loved Millie as a daughter and she knew she was hard-working and trustworthy. She told everyone that no one could sell her hats or wear them, as well as Millie.

Millie wore long, pink ribbons down the front of her dress and she carried fresh, pink rosebuds. Mary Rose stood right by her at the altar. She had a pink dress and she wore pink ribbons, in her long dark curls. Mr. Joe was very handsome in his new, dark blue suit. Toffie was the "best man." He wore his church suit. Even though they were doing very well, in the coal-hauling business, he would not buy a new suit. He had his reasons. Still he looked very handsome.

Mr. Joe insisted the family have a picture taken now that he was officially part of the family. He wanted to see that picture every day. There would be one for Joseph too. It was very hard for little Joey to sit still, but he was quiet once he was in Naaj's arms. They made a handsome picture. What a fine party they had at Joseph's house, with all their family and friends. There was plenty to eat. Na'am insisted that they all take some food home with them. She knew the lean days were not quite over for everyone. She filled the plates generously.

Mr. Joe had hired the old lady who lived next door. He asked her to clean his little house. It must shine for his bride. Jerry had moved out to the barn. He had made a comfortable room and a warm bed out of a back area, by the window. He even hung a blanket up to make a door. He could not sleep there in winter, but for now it was fine. It was cooler there. He was happy these days, but he knew he had to think of his own future. He was saving his pay almost every week.

Mr. Joe took his bride proudly, into his house. He could hardly believe that this beautiful girl was his wife. He knew he was fairly older than Millie, but he was sure he could be a good husband to her. Millie loved Mr. Joe. She was ready in her heart, to love him always and to make him a good wife and a good home. She could hardly wait to begin. She would put flowers on the window sills. She had made beautiful lace pieces for the tables. She planned to work at the hat shop until she was going to have a baby. She wanted children and Mr. Joe wanted a family too.

Before they went to bed, Millie gave Mr. Joe a tiny box. It was wrapped neatly and had a little white seal, that held the wrappings together. The dealer at the pawn shop had sold her a little, gold, tie pin, with a few seed pearls along the edge of it. It was quite handsome. Mr. Joe could not believe that Millie would spend her hard-earned money on him. He would have to buy a tie. He kissed her smiling face gently.

Mr. Joe went into the kitchen, where he lifted an old cigar box from under a loose board in the corner. "Millie, I have no wedding gift for you, except this. I want you to do whatever you wish with it. You have done me a great honor, by becoming my wife even though you believed I was poor. I want you to know that YOU are what makes me rich. I want you to be happy always."

Millie sat on the edge of the bed, a little closer to Mr. Joe. She opened the box. It was just an old box, but she said nothing. She would tell him it was wonderful no matter what was in it. Millie opened the lid and almost dropped it. It was filled with money. The bills were tied with string and placed on top of each other, in neat little piles. It had more bills than Mrs. Janeski's strong box.

"Mr. Joe, how have you come by this?" Millie was becoming concerned. "My dear little wife, I have saved for many years. Now it is for you. You see at first, it was to bring my dear mama here to America, but she is in heaven. I became used to saving every week and I needed very little for myself. My house is all paid up and then I even gave much away in the hard times, but now it is for you." Millie was astounded. She wrapped the box in a dish towel and gave it back to Mr. Joe, in a hasty movement. "Hide this Mr. Joe and tomorrow we will take it to the bank. It must not stay here." He replaced the old board. He took Millie into his arms most tenderly.

Joseph was dead! His fellow colleagues carefully carried him home, in the Dean's automobile, with their coats over his body. It was too late for them to call the doctor.

Joseph had finished teaching for the day and was collecting his books and papers, to carry home when he slowly fell to the wooden floor. He was clutching his chest. He did not utter a sound. One of his students had come back to retrieve his forgotten lunch pail. He ran yelling and crying, to the professor still reading, in the next school room. Na'am and the children never got to tell him they loved him one more time, or even good-bye.

Na'am missed her husband more than anyone realized. She would climb up to the attic bedroom at night and touch his books, and hold his old slippers near to her heart. She showed no one her tears. She would sleep in their bed and feel his arms around her. Yet every morning she would get up, wash herself, comb her hair, put on one of her two freshly washed house dresses, and go down the stairs saying, "Good morning my children." She would look at Mary Rose first. Mary Rose reminded her of Joseph more than the others. She had his gentle ways. When Na'am had a question Mary Rose would look up with "his look." Oh yes, Na'am saw Joseph in each one of her children and she looked for him in them, everyday. The little children and baby kept her busy. Her "baking orders" were getting bigger. The days were going by somehow. Na'am was always kind; but she didn't smile anymore.

Na'am had been saving money for Joseph. She wanted him to see the doctor in Boston. Her oldest daughter Jennie had moved to a little house of her own. Jennie and Tom were going to have a baby. She had sent a letter for Joseph and Na'am to come. They must stay with them, while her father would be seen at the hospital. Na'am didn't have enough money saved yet, and now it was too late.

Jennie asked that Mary Rose come to visit. She longed to see her mother, sisters, and brothers. But she knew well that it would be impossible, for all of them to come. Perhaps Mary Rose would help her with her first baby soon to be born. Na'am decided Mary Rose should go to Boston. Perhaps Tom would find time to take Mary Rose to see the fine school there. This school took only women and Na'am liked that because she thought it must be a serious place of study. Joseph wanted his children to go to college. Mary Rose had a fine mind. She was a good student. Besides, what else could Na'am do with the money she had been saving? She wanted to do something special with it. If she could not save Joseph perhaps she could make his dream come true. One of his children would go to college. She worked even harder.

Toffie wanted to talk with his mother alone. They went for a walk to the little park not far, from their house. "Mother, I must go away." "What! Toffie, would you leave me too?" My heart, do not do this I beg you," cried Na'am. Tears began to run down her face. She was no longer young. Life's hardships were starting to show in her face.

"Mother try to understand, I did not get to say goodbye to father and if I don't get away, I will die of grief. I am still very young and I have not seen anything, of the world. I have only a high school education and I want to do more than haul coal all my life. I don't want to go to college, that is for Mary to do." "You must not join the army, son! They came to take all the men and boys from our towns for that! Most never came back." "OK, little mother, I will join the Navy and be safe"....Toffie laughed, and wiped his mother's face with his sleeve. "Mother, there is talk of war and I must do my part. This is a wonderful country not like your town at all. I have been happy here. It's only fair that I go. Besides I want to go. I promise to send you letters and presents, from everywhere. I want to see everything. I even hope to see where you and father lived as children. I will see to it that you receive my pay too. I will keep only a little. Jerry must come and do my job with Naaj. He needs a home too. Please mother, I must go." Na'am could not stop weeping! She looked at his young, eager face. How can I bear this too, my Lord God, she thought.

Mary Rose was in Boston but she would be home soon as she must be home in time, for the start of school. She would be a senior this year. Her older sister had a baby girl born beautiful and healthy. Jennie, her sister wanted to call her new baby Maria, however, Mary Rose decided that since she was the Godmother the baby would be named Mary. Little Mary seemed to agree. Toffie planned to leave as soon as possible. He wanted to say good-bye to Mary Rose. Time was getting short.

Mary Rose pushed the door open with her foot. She was carrying her suitcase and presents for everyone. Her older sister had taken her shopping, in every one of the beautiful shops, in downtown Boston. Mary Rose didn't have a penny left. But, she could hardly wait to see everyone. She missed them all. She missed her mother, Na'am most of all.

"Oh Toffie, how can you leave us? Don't you know how we will all miss you?" Toffie looked more handsome than ever, in his Navy uniform. Mary Rose was secretly proud of her brother. She knew his heart could not be happy, in this little coal town until he had spread his wings first. She knew too, that it would hurt her mother to see him go. Mary Rose had a real friend in her brother. He understood her and she understood him. Besides, he made her laugh.

"You must write to us and to mother everyday! I will tell you my final secret, until you come home! Are you ready?" Mary Rose whispered into his ear that mother could read. Toffie was astonished. "How do you know that," he asked? "Well, I was reading that old children's book to little Joey, Barbara, and Philip. Mother corrected me. I don't think she realized she had done it. See if you can catch her at it. She reads everything; even signs and old newspapers. Don't say that I told you, you must not let on, that you know. It's her very own secret. Ok? and Toffie, I love you my dearest, dear brother." "Mary Rose, do not be afraid and little sister. I will write to you and tell you about everything I see. I will address a letter to mother too, with her own dear name on it. Won't SHE be surprised then!"

CHAPTER 7

The Best Surprise of All

T offie had completed his training and he had his
ship. Before they knew it, time had gone by and he
had sailed overseas. Naaj and Jerry drove the coal truck
everyday, but Sunday. Jerry had the tiny back bedroom in
Na'am's house now. They fit a small bed in there and he had
his own bureau, with a mirror. Mr. Joe still kept a sharp eye
on him. But there was no need. Jerry was a good boy. He
had quit school. But, he was his own person now. He was
earning a good living and he was saving, as Mr. Joe had
taught him. He realized that it was important for his
future. Jerry loved Na'am and her family. He felt at home
right away. He was most courteous to everyone, but he
would find excuses to visit Loretta and Little Sweetheart.

Sometimes he would take them out for a walk, to
the little park. Then they would go to the drug store for ice
cream sundaes. Jerry was about three years younger than
Loretta, but the hardships they had endured during their
youth gave them quiet talks to share. They were both doing
so much better these days, that it gave them
something about which to be hopeful. They both loved and
delighted in little Lora who kept them busy, but they were
falling in love with each other slowly, but surely.

Mary Rose was in high school, it was her last year home, before she would go to college. She would stay with her sister Jennie and Tom and baby Mary in Boston. They had plenty of room and Mary Rose could help with the baby. She mentioned it often so her mother would get used to the idea. She wanted to be a teacher as her father was before her; only she would teach American History. She didn't realize that when she talked about this it made Na'am hopeful, as she would have kept her pledge to Joseph that at least one of their children would go to college. Na'am was ready for Mary Rose's future. She was not ready for Naaj and Jennie and the children's' future.

Jennie's mother was very ill. Her father wanted her to come home and take care of her mother. He would give Naaj a good job in his store, at first. He would eventually give both of them the store, if they wanted it. His own sons had careers of their own and were not interested in running it anymore. It would belong to Jennie and Naaj. It was a good future for them and the children. But, they would have to live in Scranton near her mother and father. They needed her.

Na'am was going to be alone. She hated the thought of it. Her house would soon be paid off in full and there was only a small balance owed on the truck. Jerry would haul the coal, take a good paycheck for himself, and give a portion of the profit to Na'am. The truck still belonged to Naaj and Toffie. Na'am continued to bake her bread. It was delicious and the people on the hill would order most of it. She continued to give the children, who came to the window thick slices of bread and milk. The penny dish was washed and put away. The little faces sometimes changed, but they still came. Hunger was never far away for some.

Millie had a full life now, but she loved her mother, and would come by to visit her. She and Mr. Joe would walk with her, to church, on Sunday mornings. The house began to have echoes. Na'am would make supper for Jerry. She treated him as her own son. He was grateful and happy. But lately, he was spending more and more time at Loretta's house. She thought they would marry soon.

One Sunday morning after Mass and breakfast Mr. Joe was reading the paper, in Na'am's front parlor. He was hoping the telephone would ring. He loved to answer it. Millie and he had purchased the hat shop from Mrs. Janeski, with the cigar box money. Mrs. Janeski and Millie made the hats in the back room talking, while they worked. They had two young girls working out front. Millie was good to them.

The people on the hill had discovered the wonderful shop, once Millie put tea and biscuits in there, to be eaten, as they talked and tried on the hats. Millie put a few clothes in the shop, too. Her fashion sense delighted the ladies. Millie charged fair prices to her neighbors, however, she would sell her expensive things, to the ladies from the hill.

Mr. Joe had seen a telephone for the first time, on his peddling rounds. He insisted on having one in his house so he could call Millie everyday. He was always thrilled to hear her voice. She would say, "Hello Mr. Joe, dear!"

He made Millie put one in her shop. Now business became even better. The ladies would call Millie for various fashionable hats and to ask her advice on matching certain outfits. If Millie didn't have an item, she would make it, or order it. She would never say she didn't carry it.

Millie insisted on putting a phone in her Mother's house too, ever since Naaj and Jennie moved to Scranton and Mary moved to Boston, for school especially, because of Toffie. Millie wanted to talk to her mother every evening as well. She worried that her mother was too lonely. Mr. Joe picked up the ringing phone. His face turned ashen! He called to Millie with a strangled voice. Millie knew something was wrong and she came running out of Na'am's kitchen, where they were washing the dishes. The Naval Officer on the phone wanted to talk to Na'am. Na'am came to the phone and her hand reached for it. She was trembling. Na'am did not like the new telephone. She knew it was bad news. It was! Toffie had been wounded by knife wounds. He had gone on shore with his friends, to explore the town. It was considered a safe place for U.S. servicemen. He was back on board the ship in "sickbay" however, the ship was headed to another port where he and others would be taken to a hospital, for recovery. It was serious. An officer would be coming very soon to talk to Na'am. He would be able to tell her more.

Na'am sat by her window in the big bedroom. The sun felt good on her face and arms. The tears slipped down her face. She did not even notice them. She prayed, "Father, Thy will be done. But I beg you to spare this good son who has given Joseph; his father and me happiness, and even laughter and joy." She tried to remember a time when Toffie had been naughty, hateful, or mean as a child. She could not remember one time. All she remembered was a little, yellow flower in his church jacket. She remembered him dancing with the girls and laughing, and making them laugh. She remembered how he would play jokes on her. Pulling her apron strings so her apron would fall off her waist, especially, when her arms were covered with soap suds, and she could not swat him. She sighed from deep sorrow as mothers have done, from the beginning of time.

72

The postman had come. Na'am looked through the few bills that had arrived. Suddenly, she froze. Here was a letter from Toffie addressed to her. Na'am called Millie on that dreaded telephone. Millie said, "Mother I will come right now. Don't be afraid." Millie left the shop and hurried away.

They sat down at the kitchen table. Na'am opened the letter very slowly and carefully. It read: "Hello Mother, I am writing this letter directly to you! Naughty woman, I know you can read! So smile because we are all very proud of you. I have a wonderful surprise for you. A few weeks ago, I went off ship with some friends and we got a car to drive, into the countryside. We crossed into the country where you and father were born. I found your old house! I found that your sister Raja had five sons! Two years ago the army came for them and took four of them away. We found the younger son tilling the fields, by himself. He is married and has children. Your sister Raja lives with them now. My uncle was struck down by the army men as he was trying to stop them, from taking their sons.

The army had even taken over their house for a while and they had to live hidden away with friends, in the city for a time. But, news came as the army moved out, and they were able to get the house back. Auntie Raja fears that she will never see her boys again. I believe she is right. She has had a very hard time of it mother. Whenever my buddies and I got some time off from the ship, we went to help them. The house is in fairly livable condition now. The field is planted and growing. We brought them food and many things they really, truly needed. Before I left them the last time, we all pitched in and gave them enough money, to help them for a time. I have some good pals.

We played with the children and mother we have had freshly baked bread, exactly like yours! The guys love to go with me. They made us all feel so welcome. It is amazing, because this auntie talks in your voice and makes me laugh, as you did. She gives me fresh bread still hot from the oven, with jam on it. She even taps me on the cheek as you used to do. Two days from now will be our last day in this port. Our ship is leaving soon. The weeks have flown by.

Auntie Raja said to tell you that, the Prince's family and all his people have scattered and most are dead. She knows that he and your parents have gone to heaven. She said to tell you she still remembers your childhood together and she still loves you.

Mother, in five weeks you must go to New York. Make Millie take you on Mr. Joe's horse, if you have to. Take the bus or the truck, but you must get there. Please promise me you will do this, just for me. You must go to the dock and stay there. I have arranged for a large package for you, but you must pick it up yourself. Please wear your Sunday church hat. I love you, mother. I will be home when this war is over. I can't wait to tease you about your secret, reading lessons with father. Love, Your Son, Toffie."

Na'am looked at the date on the letter. It was written the day before he was attacked. He and his friends had been hurrying back to the ship. They had just returned the car they had hired, for the week-end. They were walking and talking to each other not paying attention, to their surroundings when it happened. It was very crowded as they neared the ship. Suddenly people were screaming and running away. Four sailors were lying on the street and dock. One was already dead. They were all rushed on board the ship. The police sirens and military police were everywhere. The attackers were gone melting easily, into the running crowds. But, he is alive! He is alive, thought Na'am. She went before the crucifix to pray.

Should we still go to the dock, asked Millie? I'm sure it would be of no use. It is a long trip from Shenandoah to New York. Perhaps Toffie was not able to send his promised present after all. Na'am would go even if she had to walk! Even if there were no reason to go! She would do as her son begged her to do, in his letter! She hurried to the bus station, to buy her ticket. Millie called Mary Rose on the telephone. Mary Rose said mother should go. She would take a leave from school, for that day and get on the very early bus, to New York. She would meet mother at the dock. Mary Rose told Millie not to worry, that she would stay with Mother as long as it took, to sort this all out and then see to it, that she was safely on the bus home, by night time. Millie breathed a sigh of relief. She could not leave her shop, and she would come afterwards to bake the bread, for Na'am's orders. For now, she would try to teach Na'am about traveling, in the big city, all by herself.

"Mary Rose! Mary Rose!" Na'am shouted across the crowded docks to her daughter. They flew into each other's arms. "How beautiful you are, Mary Rose!" "Yes, Mother I am very happy at school. Also mother, I have met someone! He is handsome, kind, and a little wild." Na'am looked more closely at Mary Rose. Yes, she could see Mary Rose was in love as her eyes were happy and shining. "Mary Rose you must finish what was promised to your father." "Mother, it is what I want too. Besides, it's quite good for wild ones to wait! Now tell me all about your bus trip and tell me what this is all about, and tell me everything."

They sat down on one of the benches breathless, with the excitement, of being together again. Na'am was elated from the bus ride. She hadn't realized how beautiful, and how big everything was. The trees, the cars, the people, and the buildings were like a world apart from the little town, where she had lived all these years. She suddenly understood Toffie's longing to leave their little home. There was so much to see.

She had been lonely in her big empty house. She missed her family all around her. She prayed for Toffie every hour. But she knew what all mothers know, that their children will grow up and go away. Still just for today she would be happy, to be with Mary Rose. Na'am opened her large bulky purse. She took out the now battered old black hat and pressed it on her neatly, combed, and rolled, gray hair. They both laughed! "Mary Rose, we must look for my package from Toffie." "Mother, perhaps we should ask at the Port Master's office. We really don't know what we are looking for. Perhaps he can help us."

The people were gradually thinning out as they talked. Many people had been shouting, hugging, and milling around as their loved ones arrived, but now there were few people left. Mary Rose looked around and around, but Na'am suddenly stood up, as still as a stone statue. She stared at a woman approaching her. She couldn't move! The lady who was walking towards her was wearing a black shawl, over her white hair. She wore a long, black dress, it covered her ankles. She was carrying a loaf of bread. She had two small children with her. They were all very frightened and holding hands tightly. The children looked exactly alike. They were twins.

Na'am began to cry. But these tears were tears of joy! The woman cried out in a scream and ran towards Na'am. They embraced and would not let go of each other.

It was Raja! "I thought I would never see you again my sister," she said in her native tongue. Na'am answered in the same language, "God is good, God is so good!" Mary Rose was astounded; she had never heard her mother speak anything, but English even though she had an accent. What a pretty sound to hear her native language. This woman was her aunt. She just knew it.

"Who are these angels?" asked Na'am at last. My sister we have come to you, to beg for a home. It was their only way to freedom. They are my grandsons. They are of course, my only remaining son's children. Never again must they be taken away by the armies. It broke my son's and daughter-in-law's hearts, to let them go. It is their chance for freedom! Will you accept us?" "Your son Toffie said we must come!" Na'am began to weep again. She said, "My sister, you know my answer!" Mary Rose stood there bewildered by the scene. Na'am laughed and translated for Mary Rose and back again for Raja.

They must all go to lunch in a real restaurant and afterwards they would sleep, on the bus ride home. Mary Rose would take a different bus back to Boston. She would have a wonderful story to tell Jennie and Tom.

When they finally reached Na'am's quiet kitchen, Raja sat down on a chair. She inhaled the smells that were so familiar to her. She told the children they were home now. The children sat very still, on the floor not sure what to do. Na'am gave them some biscuits with apple jam and milk. Then she brought out an old box of toys left behind by little Joey. It was very late, but no one could sleep just yet.

Finally, Raja rose up from the chair. She took the loaf of bread she had carried all that way. It was wrapped safely in her shawl. She asked Na'am not to be afraid. She raised the hard bread and hit it against the kitchen table. It cracked in half and the crumbs were flying everywhere. Inside was a little cloth. Raja gently pulled and twisted it out of the hard bread. She unwrapped it and gave it to Na'am. There before her eyes, in her hands was that which she had been trying to remember, for so long. It was hand carved and worn very smooth. It was a wooden figure of the Madonna with Her arms up-stretched. Two tears made of tiny rubies, on Her face. Na'am took the figure into the living room and tapped a small nail, into the wall just below and a bit to the left of the crucifix. When she hung the Madonna up, the Blessed Mother, Mary was looking at Her Son, Jesus, reaching her arms to him. Now she remembered! Both figures were together just like that hanging, in her grandmother's cottage where she and Raja had their first lessons, in baking bread.

"Welcome home Raja, my dear sister! Come, I will show you where you and the little ones will sleep." She led them into the big bedroom. She kissed her sister's tired, wrinkled face and she kissed the little ones heartily. She brought out an extra blanket and placed it on the big bed. Na'am was smiling once again.

Na'am was still smiling. She turned back to the kitchen. She put on her apron. She had bread to set and let rise. Soon it would be morning. There would be laughter in her house and heart once more. "God is so good," she thought.

ABOUT THE AUTHOR

I have been writing all my life. The library was around the corner from my home, in the South End of Boston, Massachusetts. In the 1940's, this was where I spent a lot of my childhood reading and dreaming. My teachers, mother, and dad were a great source of knowledge and I received a good education from them. Being the eldest of eight children, I had a lot of practical experiences as well, while helping to care for my younger siblings.

Drawing on my childhood memories, this author remembers grandparents and parents discussing the old ways around the kitchen table, or while sitting in the parlor. Growing up in circumstances of need, but never being told so. I truly, never knew I was in any need, all thanks to my mother Mary-Rose.

Drawing on truth for many parts of this story I realize that I grew up, with a wealth of love and valuable traditions. Seeing the world today I long for children to have the same love and warmth in every home and I hope and pray they will have the love that all children deserve.

Being a wife, mother, and grandmother now, and living near the ocean, I love every minute of it. I am writing other short stories in hope that they will inspire others and especially, children to write and create their own traditions.
                    Dolores Kruzona